11/21

D0457845

THE LAIR OF TANABRAX

THE LAIR OF TANABRAX

By Tracey West

Random House New York

LEGO, the LEGO logo, the Brick and Knob configurations, the Minifigure and NINJAGO are trademarks and/or copyrights of the LEGO Group. ©2021 The LEGO Group. All rights reserved.

 Manufactured under licence granted to AMEET Sp. z o.o. by the LEGO Group.

AMEET Sp. z o.o.
Nowe Sady 6, 94-102 Łódź—Poland
ameet@ameet.eu
www.ameet.eu

www.LEGO.com

Published in the United States by Random House Children's Books, a division of Penguin Random House LLC, 1745 Broadway, New York, NY 10019, and in Canada by Penguin Random House Canada Limited, Toronto. Random House and the colophon are registered trademarks of Penguin Random House LLC.

rhcbooks.com

ISBN 978-0-593-38143-4 (trade) — ISBN 978-0-593-38144-1 (lib. bdg.)
ISBN 978-0-593-38145-8 (ebook)

Printed in the United States of America

10 9 8 7 6 5 4 3 2 1

First Edition 2021

CONTENTS

 **Prologue**

Master Wu and the six ninja strolled through a village outside Ninjago City.

"Let me get this straight," Jay said. "We came all the way to this village to stop a ring of chicken thieves and it turns out it was just a bunch of foxes?"

"Most of the time, the simplest explanation is the correct one," Master Wu said.

"I don't mind coming here," Jay said. "It's nice to have a break from training."

Kai looked at the small houses, surrounded by rice fields. "Not much to do here, though."

Cole sniffed the air. "Are those mooncakes I smell?" He followed his nose away from the others.

"Cole, we've got to get back to the monastery!" Lloyd called out, but Cole didn't turn around.

Nya laughed. "I'm sure Cole's on the scent of something good. Let's check it out!"

They followed Cole through the twisting village streets to the town marketplace. Colorful decorations hung from the trees.

"Those look like . . . turnips?" Jay asked.

Zane scanned his database. "On this day every year, this village holds a Turnip Festival. There are games of chance, entertainment, and different kinds of food made from turnips, including their famous turnip donuts."

"*That's* what I smelled!" Cole said. "I have got to try those."

Lloyd turned to Master Wu. "Do we have time?"

"I suppose we at least have time for a cup of tea or two," the ninja master replied.

"Cool!" Jay said. "We should check out that traveling puppet show over there. It looks like lots of fun."

"Puppets? NO PUPPETS!" Master Wu said sharply. The ninja all froze and looked at him with surprise.

"Please?" Nya asked. "I'd love to see the puppets just for a few minutes."

Master Wu shook his head. "Isn't there something else you'd like to do? I think I see a turnip-toss game over there. Anything but puppets!"

"Um, not to be disrespectful, Master Wu, but what do you have against puppets?" Kai asked.

A cloud came over Master Wu's face. "It is a long story," he said. "But one you must hear. Let us sit under this tree and I will tell you."

"Wait! I'll get us some donuts first!" Cole said, and he hurried away. Master Wu sat cross-legged at the base of the tree and the rest of the ninja joined him.

4

"Master Wu, does this story take place when you and your brother, Garmadon, were young, and your father sent you on that long journey?" Nya asked. "You know, the quest to find a special healing tea for Garmadon."

Master Wu nodded. "Indeed. And we were very young at that time."

"You never told us how that journey ended, Master Wu," Kai said.

"All in due time," Master Wu replied, stroking his long beard. "It was a long adventure, and quite an important one. And this story is part of it."

Cole came running back. "Turnip donuts for everyone!" he said. "And I got you some tea, Master Wu."

The old man gratefully took the cup from him and sipped the tea.

"Where to begin," Wu said. "Garmadon and I had been traveling for several days when we came upon a village just like this one. . . ."

Chapter 1
The Village

"I spy . . . something green," Wu said.

"Seriously?" Garmadon asked, rolling his eyes. "This is the third time you've spied something green."

"Well, we've been walking through woods and fields," Wu pointed out matter-of-factly. "Almost everything is green."

Garmadon sighed. "Fine," he said. "Is it the grass?"

"No," Wu replied.

Garmadon pointed. "That tree over there?"

"Nope," Wu answered.

"What about that tree over there?" Garmadon asked. "Is that it?"

Wu shook his head. "Uh-uh."

Garmadon pointed behind him. "That one?" he asked loudly, agitated.

"No," Wu said, grinning with the anticipation of winning. "Do you give up?"

"Sure," Garmadon said.

Wu pointed to another tree. "*That* one! That tree!"

"I almost had it," his brother replied flatly. "Do we have to keep playing this game?"

"No, but I can't think of a better one," Wu said. "It's been five days since we left the Temple of Felis. We've talked about everything we can talk about. And I've sang every song I can remember."

"I know. I heard you sing them *all*." Garmadon kicked a stone on the path in front of him. "I don't know why we're still on this stupid journey, anyway. I don't need any tea to 'fix' me. There's nothing wrong with me."

The boys' father, the First Spinjitzu Master, had started them on this quest weeks ago. He was worried about the darkness he'd seen rising in Garmadon. He said that there was a tea plant growing on the shores of the northern ocean that could fix his son.

"Mm-hmm," Wu said. He didn't want to argue with Garmadon, but he thought their father was right. Something hadn't been quite right with his brother ever since that day when they were just kids and he'd been bitten by a serpent.

Wu and Garmadon had always been opposites in many ways. As a young boy, white-haired Wu had been impatient and a little reckless. His dark-haired brother, Garmadon, had been thoughtful and caring. But after Wu had stolen their father's scrolls of Forbidden Spinjitzu, Wu changed. He became the responsible one, and Garmadon started to take more risks.

That was what led Garmadon to climb over the wall of the monastery one day, where the snake had bit him. And ever since that bite, Wu had noticed a change in his brother. Garmadon would burst into sudden, stormy moods and flashes of anger. This frightened Wu, and if the tea could help Garmadon, he would travel to the scariest regions of Ninjago to get it for him.

"We should just turn back," Garmadon continued. "Turn back and tell Father we're not going on some wild chase for no reason."

"You and I both know that won't work," Wu said. "We both want to become great masters of Spinjitzu, don't we? We can't do that without Father's training. I'm sure it won't take us too much longer to find the plant."

"Mm-hmm," Garmadon replied, and Wu knew that was his brother's way of admitting that Wu was right. Garmadon let the subject drop, so Wu continued with the game.

"Your turn," Wu said. "What do you spy?"

Garmadon stopped and squinted into the distance. "I spy several plumes of chimney smoke. It's a village!"

"Hey, you're supposed to let me guess," Wu said.

Garmadon rolled his eyes. "You're missing the point, brother.

We're almost out of food and we haven't slept on a soft bed in a long time. A village is just what we need."

"You're right!" Wu said, and he broke into a run. "Last one there is a slimy snake!"

Garmadon and Wu charged down the path and reached the village at the same time. Small homes with neat gardens lined the stone streets. The brothers could see a marketplace in the center of the village, and they headed there.

But as they passed by the houses, Wu noticed something strange. A mother playing with her two kids stared at the boys, then shook her head sadly. They walked past another house and saw a man staring at them from a window. When they passed the next house, a man was watering flowers outside.

"Hello there," Wu greeted him. "What's the name of this village? We've traveled a long way, and—"

"There's nothing much to see here," the man replied. "You'd best be on your way."

"But we're tired and hungry," Garmadon said.

The man frowned. "Like I said, you need to keep moving." And he went back to watering his flowers.

Wu and Garmadon looked at each other.

"Are you getting a weird vibe from this place?" Wu asked.

Garmadon nodded. "Yeah, nobody here seems to be very friendly." Then he sniffed the air. "Mmm! What's that delicious smell?"

Wu sniffed, too. "I don't know, but weird villagers or not, I want to find out!"

They followed their noses to the marketplace. There were small stands of people selling fruit, vegetables, bread, and cooked foods, like dumplings and soup.

"Dumplings!" both brothers cried together. Without another word, they made their way to the dumpling stand.

"Let's order a dozen of each kind," Garmadon said, his mouth watering.

"I would, but we're almost out of money," Wu informed him.

"How much do we have?" Garmadon asked.

Wu took some coins out of his pockets and looked at the sign on the stand. "Enough for one dumpling," he said.

Garmadon nodded to the gray-haired woman behind the counter, who was placing dumplings in a bamboo basket to steam.

"We'd like one dumpling, please," he said.

The woman raised an eyebrow. "One dumpling?"

"That's what I said," Garmadon answered. "Is there a problem with that?"

"Only if you continue to be rude to an old lady," the woman shot back. "One dumpling is kind of a

strange order. People talk about my dumplings all over Ninjago. Nobody ever orders just one. They order six, or twelve, or a hundred!"

Wu held out his coins. "We can only afford one dumpling."

She shook her head and clicked her tongue, but then she opened another steamer basket and used chopsticks to pick up a single dumpling.

"No, not that one!" Garmadon cried. "Can you choose the biggest one?"

"Really?" the woman asked. "They're all the same size."

"No, they're not," Garmadon insisted, and he pointed. "That one's a little bigger."

The dumpling seller was not convinced. "It is not."

"Just give us the big one!" Garmadon's voice got loud.

Wu sighed and put a hand on his brother's arm. "It's okay, Garmadon," he said soothingly. "We can get a bunch of carrots instead. They'll be easier to share."

Then he heard a voice behind them.

"Grandma, give them a plate of dumplings."

The brothers turned to see a girl who looked to be about their age, with short brown hair.

"Thank you," Wu said. "My name's Wu, and this is my brother, Garmadon."

The girl smiled. "I'm Hana, and that's my grandmother."

"Call me Obachan," the woman said gruffly, and

she piled eight dumplings on a plate and passed it to them.

Garmadon looked at Hana. "Why are you doing this? You don't even know us."

Hana shrugged. "You look hungry. And Grandma and I like to feed people."

"We've been traveling for weeks," Wu explained. "And we're running out of supplies. Do you know of anyone looking for an extra hand? Maybe we could stay the night here and do some work in the morning to earn money so we can buy more food."

"You do not want to stay the night here," Obachan said dryly.

Wu frowned. "Another guy told us that, too."

"Why can't we stay?" Garmadon asked. "It's not a bad little village."

"It is an excellent village!" Obachan snapped. "But it is not a good time for visitors to stay here."

"I don't get it," Wu said. "You have great food, and the flowers are in bloom. If we weren't on a journey, we'd stay for a few days."

Obachan looked at her granddaughter.

"These are nice boys," the woman said. "Should we tell them?"

Hana nodded. "Our village is in danger, and they should know it."

Garmadon perked up. "Danger? What danger?"

"People have been disappearing," Hana explained. "My own brother went missing two weeks ago. Some said he left to move to the city, but he wouldn't have left us without saying goodbye. More people have vanished since then. The villagers swear that—"

"Enough, Hana," Obachan said. "That is all these boys need to know. They should leave before night falls."

"And where will they go?" Hana asked. "The next village is nearly a day's journey away. They'll be safer here."

"Well, we're ninja and we're not afraid," Garmadon informed them, and he spun into a dashing ninja kick to prove it.

Hana looked them over. They each wore a gi— loose pants with a lightweight shirt on top tied in front, perfect for ninja battles.

"Is that what you are?" she asked. "I wondered why you were wearing pajamas."

"These aren't pajamas!" Garmadon snapped, his voice rising.

"Yes, we're ninja," Wu said. "And my brother's right. We're not afraid to stay here. Do you know of any place we could sleep tonight?"

"You could sleep in my brother's room, right, Grandma?" Hana asked.

Obachan snorted.

"Come on, Grandma. If they are what they claim to be, they'll be fine. And maybe they'll even help keep us safe, too," Hana added.

Obachan finally agreed.

"It's settled!" Hana said. "You're staying with us. Now eat your dumplings before they get cold."

The brothers didn't argue. They quickly downed the delicious dumplings. When the sun began to set, they helped Hana and Obachan pack up the market stand and brought it back to their cottage. The pretty white house had a flower garden in the back. Hana led them inside and up to a room on the second floor.

"There's only one bed, but there are extra blankets, so one of you can have the floor," she said.

"Thank you," Wu said. "We really appreciate it."

"Yeah, thanks," Garmadon echoed. Then he jumped onto the bed. "Mine!"

"No fair!" Wu jumped in next to him. "You can't just call it like that."

"Can too," Garmadon said.

"Well, this bed is really comfortable. I'm not leaving," Wu said. "We can share."

"Fine," Garmadon said.

"Fine," Wu echoed.

The brothers squeezed onto the bed, back to back. But as tired as they were, they couldn't seem to fall asleep. Wu kept running the conversation with Hana and Obachan over and over in his mind.

"Do you really think something weird is happening in this village?" Wu asked.

"Probably not," Garmadon said. "This place is in the middle of nowhere. I bet everyone really is just leaving for the big city."

"Hana didn't think that was what happened," Wu pointed out.

"Well, she probably just doesn't want to believe it," Garmadon said with a yawn.

Then the five days of walking caught up to them, and the brothers drifted off to sleep.

Chapter 2
A Creepy Secret

Wu dreamed.

He and Garmadon found the tea plant—a huge plant with leaves that wriggled like snakes. They cut the plant at the stalk and stuffed it into a tea kettle full of water. Then they boiled the tea, and Wu poured some into a cup and gave it to Garmadon.

"Drink up, brother!" Wu said. "You'll be better in no time."

Garmadon sipped. Wu waited.

"Did it work?" Wu asked. "Is the evil gone?"

Garmadon didn't answer. His eyes glazed over red. They began to glow. Then Garmadon began to grow bigger . . . and bigger . . . and bigger . . .

"Oh, no! Brother, what's happening?" Wu cried. "Somebody, help! Help! Help!"

Wu woke up shaking. He looked over at his brother, who was snoring peacefully next to him. Then he heard:

"Help! Help!"

That sound was no dream—it was coming from outside! Wu shook Garmadon awake.

"What is it?" Garmadon asked groggily.

"Something's wrong!" Wu ran to the window, and Garmadon followed him.

Outside, a group of what looked like kids—or were they tiny men?—were carrying a man more than twice their size down the street.

"Help! They've got me!" the man yelled.

Wu jumped out the window.

"Ninjaaaaaaaaaaago!"

Garmadon followed Wu. The two began to whirl like tornadoes, and they hit the ground like spinning tops. They crashed into the group of tiny men, knocking them over like bowling pins.

The man they'd been carrying fell to the ground with a thud. The little men charged at Garmadon and

Wu. Five of them grabbed Garmadon by the legs and pulled him down.

"Hey, get off me!" Garmadon cried, pushing them off him.

Six more attacked Wu from behind, hitting him behind the knees. Wu stumbled and then twirled around and hit one with a martial arts kick. The little man flew into the air and Garmadon caught him.

"Gotcha!" he yelled. Then he gasped and dropped him. "It's a puppet!"

The dropped puppet jumped back to his feet and started kicking Garmadon in the ankles.

"Hey, quit it!" Garmadon yelled. He kicked the puppet, sending it flying.

"What do you mean, 'it's a puppet'?" Wu asked. He picked up one of the tiny men who was attacking him with kicks and punches.

The kidnapper in his hands had clearly been carved out of wood. His eyes were blue glass marbles. Then the eyes blinked and the puppet's mouth began to

move. Wu let go of him, shocked and surprised. The puppet ran off. The other puppets followed him.

Wu looked at Garmadon. "I don't get it! Those were definitely living puppets, right?"

Garmadon nodded. "It sure looks that way."

"We need to get to the bottom of this," Wu said, and they charged after the puppets, who were fleeing into the woods.

Suddenly, Wu felt his feet slipping out from under him. *Whoosh!* The next thing he knew, he was hanging upside down from a tree branch, his right ankle ensnared in a thin rope.

"YIKES!" Garmadon yelled next to him, and Wu realized that his brother had suffered the same fate.

The boys quickly swung themselves upright, grabbing on to the tree branches above them. Then they untied the snares and raced into the woods.

There was no sign of the puppets anywhere.

"We'd better head back," Wu said as they stopped to look around. "We could easily get lost here."

Garmadon frowned. "I hate to let them get away."

"From the looks of it, these weird puppets are responsible for the missing people in this village," Wu said. "Before we look for them, we need to find out

what's really been going on. I have a feeling that Hana
and Obachan didn't tell us the whole story."

Garmadon nodded, and the boys headed back
to the village. Several of the inhabitants had come
outside and gathered around the miserable man the
puppets had tried to kidnap.

Hana was one of them. She ran up to Wu and
Garmadon. "Thank you for saving Kenji!"

"About that," Garmadon began, "you could have
told us there were creepy living puppets running
around at night."

"I didn't think you'd believe us," Hana explained.

"Why don't you tell us exactly what's been going
on?" Wu asked.

Hana nodded. "Let's go inside."

Obachan had a pot of hot tea waiting for them, and she beamed when she saw the brothers.

"I don't like to be wrong, but I will always admit when I am," she said. "It's a very good thing Hana convinced me to let you stay with us. You saved our neighbor. You are truly the ninja you say you are! Now come, have some tea. Please."

They sat around the kitchen table and Obachan poured the tea. Wu suddenly remembered his dream and turned pale.

"Are you all right?" Obachan asked.

Wu shook off the creepy feeling he had. "Sure, I'm fine. Just remembering a weird dream I had last night."

Garmadon looked at his brother. "Yeah, I had a weird dream, too."

Was it the same as mine? Wu thought. "Was I in it?" he asked.

"Would you two like to discuss your dreams, or would you like to know what's been happening?" Obachan asked.

"We definitely need to know what's going on," Wu replied. "Tell us about those strange creatures that tried to kidnap Kenji. They looked like puppets carved from wood, but they were alive."

Hana nodded. "The night my brother, Shin, went missing, a little girl said she saw puppets take him. But nobody believed her. *I* didn't even believe her."

"Then, the next night, Farmer Uchida's wife was taken," Obachan continued. "His poor daughter said he followed them—but never came back."

Wu shivered. "Creepy."

"It gets even creepier," Hana said. "The next night, I saw the puppets running away with Old Man Jiro. And two of the puppets looked exactly like Farmer Uchida and his wife—only smaller. And they were wearing the same clothes they'd been taken in."

"Only smaller," Garmadon said with a smirk.

Hana shuddered. "It's not funny—it's creepy! Like someone designed those puppets to look like the people we know. I tried to go after them, but—"

"But I stopped her," Obachan interrupted. "I do not need to lose both of my grandchildren."

"Shin is not lost," Hana said. "I'm afraid to think about what might have happened to him. I know somebody is kidnapping people. And then puppets are showing up that *look* like the kidnapped people. What all that means—I'm not sure. But I'm going to find out!"

She looked at the brothers.

"Will you help me?" she asked.

"We would love to, but we're on a very important journey," Garmadon said. "We've got to leave this village tomorrow."

Hana's eyes narrowed. "But you said you were looking to do some work so you could buy supplies. Help us, and we'll give you all the supplies you need."

"You don't have to give us anything," Wu told her. "We'll help you because it's the right thing to do. Right, brother?"

Garmadon sighed. "Right," he said, and then his eyes lit up, as if he'd just hatched a really mischievous plan. "But since it's your idea to help, then you won't mind being bait."

Wu's stomach sank. If Garmadon was planning it, it couldn't be good for him. "Bait for what?"

Garmadon grinned. "Bait for the puppet trap we're going to set tomorrow night."

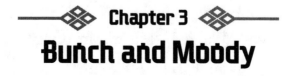

Chapter 3
Bunch and Moody

"What a beautiful night to be asleep outside!" Wu said loudly. "Out here in the garden, where anyone could kidnap me if they wanted to."

Garmadon hissed from behind the mulberry tree. "Don't be so obvious, Wu!"

Wu was lying on a cot in Obachan's flower garden, pretending to be asleep under the night sky. But he decided to add some dialogue to his performance.

"Well, you wanted me to be bait, brother," Wu shot back. "I'm just letting the puppets know that I'm an easy target."

"Too easy," Garmadon grumbled. "Now be quiet! You've got the simple job. All you have to do is pretend to sleep. I've got to try to follow you without being seen by the puppets."

"How is that harder than being handled by a bunch of super-creepy living dolls?" Wu wanted to know.

"Because you don't have to do anything except just lie there," Garmadon shot back.

"Shhhhhh!" Wu said. "I hear something."

Tap! Tap! Tap! The sound of tiny feet marching on the cobblestone road filled the night air. Then the marching stopped, and Garmadon and Wu heard two voices on the other side of the garden wall.

"This is so hard-io, Bunch!" a voice wailed. "Everyone's got their doors locked and windows closed and blocked."

"Stop whining, Moody!" the other voice scolded. "The boss-io says we'd better bring him another soul tonight-io or he'll turn us into toothpicks."

Wu hissed at Garmadon. "Are those the puppets? I didn't know they could talk!"

Garmadon peered through a hole in the garden wall. About a dozen puppets were outside on the street. Two of the puppets seemed to be leading them. One had red eyes and blue, spiky hair made of flax, and wore a blue shirt with a picture of a crying face on it.

The other had dark spiky hair, and his black shirt had a grinning face with sharp teeth. The puppets behind them stared straight ahead with blank looks in their glass eyes.

"They're puppets, all right," Garmadon hissed back. "Quite a lot of them."

The two lead puppets kept talking.

"How can we bring the boss-io a new soul if those ninja are in town, Bunch?" asked Moody, the blue-haired puppet. "We're not strong enough to fight them. Or clever enough."

He motioned to the puppet army. "This new batch of souls is about as smart-io as a pile of logs."

Wait, thought Garmadon. *Why do they keep talking about souls? I thought these puppets were just some wacky magic trick. Is there more going on?*

"You know that's how the boss-io works," Bunch reminded him. "He has to use his magic on them to control-io all them new souls. Only you and me are loyal to the boss, because we was bad-io to begin with. That's why he put you and me in charge. He knows he can count-io on the two of us. And those other puppets will listen to us."

"I'm telling you, we're going to fail the boss again-io!" Moody moaned. "We'll never be able to kidnap-io anyone tonight."

Garmadon picked up a pebble and tossed it at Wu's shoulder.

"Wu, say something!" Garmadon hissed.

"But I thought you said to be quiet?" Wu whispered.

"Forget it," Garmadon said. "Just make some noise so they find you."

Wu cleared his throat. "Oh, boy. I wonder if it's a good idea to be sleeping outside tonight. What if something happens to me?"

Garmadon heard the two puppet leaders talking in low tones. Then there was a rustling in the bushes.

Bunch entered the garden first, followed by a line of puppets. One wore a farmer's straw hat. The next wore a dress with an apron. Another one had white hair, and yet another had dark hair and a carved face that reminded Garmadon of Hana.

Could that be the farmer and his wife that Obachan told us about? Garmadon thought. *And could that dark-haired one be Hana's brother?*

Unlike Bunch, the other puppets marched stiffly. Moody, the blue-haired puppet, pushed through the bushes last.

Wu was lying perfectly still. He closed his eyes and pretended to sleep.

"It's one of those ninja guys!" Bunch said in a loud whisper. "The boss-io is going to love this!"

"Wait! What if it's a sneaky-o trap?" Moody asked nervously.

"You worry too much," Bunch said. "Come on, let's grab him!"

All the puppets rushed toward Wu, covering him like a swarm of killer bees. Garmadon had to restrain himself from stopping them. But everyone had agreed that it was important to see where the puppets were taking the kidnapped people.

"Tie him up-io!" Bunch cried, and the puppets worked quickly to wrap rope around Wu from head to toe.

"Back to the lair-io!" Moody yelled.

The puppets deftly hoisted Wu above their heads and carried him out of the garden on their tiny legs.

"Help," Wu said in a flat voice, pretending to wake and then pretending to resist. "Stop. Let me go."

Garmadon followed them swiftly and silently, staying in the shadows. The puppets carried Wu into

the woods. After a few minutes, the green juniper trees gave way to a section of woods with black bark and gnarled, twisted branches with black leaves. Garmadon shivered; the air felt colder here.

The puppets finally stopped at a round, wooden door over a hole in the ground. Bunch and Moody pulled it open and the puppets carried Wu inside. The door shut behind them.

Garmadon waited a few seconds, and when he thought it was safe, he ran to the door and opened it.

It led to a tunnel. He saw tiny puppet footprints in the dirt and followed them.

It was pitch-black in the tunnel, but he could see a dim light at the end. When he reached it, he pressed himself against the wall so he wouldn't be seen. Then he cautiously peered out to see where the tunnel led.

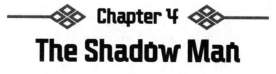

Chapter 4
The Shadow Man

A large cave opened below. More of the living puppets were there, more than Garmadon could count. The creepy creatures moved silently around with blank expressions on their faces.

Suddenly, a tall figure floated out of the shadows.

The figure looked like a man—a man with wavy black hair and white, glowing eyes. A medallion with a spiral pattern hung around his neck. He wore a long black robe, and where his feet should have been, there were four black tentacles that carried him across the floor in a wavy motion, making it look like he was hovering just above it.

Then Garmadon realized something else. . . .

It's like . . . his body is made of shadow, Garmadon thought, and he felt a sudden pang of fear. *Is Wu in real danger?*

"What soul have you brought for Tanabrax tonight?" the dark figure asked.

The puppets carried Wu over to their master, and a crooked grin spread across his face.

"You brought me a ninja," Tanabrax said. "Well done!"

"I spotted him first-io," Bunch said.

"He's lying! I did-io!" Moody cried.

Tanabrax ignored his arguing henchmen. He walked over to a workbench against the wall of the cave. As Garmadon's eyes

adjusted to the darkness, he studied the items on the bench. A pile of wooden puppets with crudely carved faces and no eyes. Stacks of material. An old sewing machine.

"How exciting! I have just the right materials to craft a ninja puppet," Tanabrax said. "He will be an excellent addition to the army."

Garmadon couldn't believe what he was hearing. He had been convinced that the puppets were just moving by magic somehow. Was this Tanabrax guy somehow actually turning *people* into *puppets*?

No, it can't be! he thought.

Wu suddenly sprang out of the arms of the puppets, shedding the rope that bound his arms. "The game is up, Tanabrax!" Wu yelled.

Garmadon shook his head. *Not yet, Wu! We need to see what this guy is really up to!*

But Wu started to launch into a spin. "Ninjaaaaa—"

Tanabrax held up the medallion around his neck, the one with the spiral pattern on it. He began to speak strange-sounding words. The medallion glowed, and the spiral pattern began to spin. Garmadon recognized the language from lessons with his father. It sounded like the ancient language of the djinn, mystical beings from the realm of Djinjago. But he didn't understand any of the words.

Wu slowly stopped, his eyes locked to the medallion. Garmadon instinctively looked away. He cautiously looked back without setting his eyes on the medallion, and saw his brother freeze.

Wu! Garmadon moved to help him, then stopped as a strange feeling came over him.

Wu is always trying to tell you what to do, a little voice said. *Just have a little fun with him and see what happens!*

Garmadon tried to push the thought out of his mind—*No, I should help him*—but it was too late.

Tanabrax held up one of the blank wooden puppets. Wu went limp. Then a tendril of white, glowing energy began to stream from Wu's mouth and into the mouth of the puppet!

Garmadon watched, transfixed with fear.

What is happening? he thought.

Then he heard a voice below him.

"Hey! It's that other ninja!"

Garmadon looked down to see the red-eyed puppet, Moody, looking up at him. Tanabrax's head snapped toward him, along with the dozens of heads in the puppet army. Garmadon thought quickly.

I can't save Wu until I know what this Tanabrax guy is up to, he thought. *And to figure that out, I'll need some help.*

He quickly picked up Moody and raced out of the tunnel.

"Let go of me!" Moody yelled frantically, waving his arms. "Bunch! Help-io!"

Garmadon kept running.

"I'll be back for you, Wu!" he called behind him.

Chapter 5
A Puppet Problem

"Let me go! I won't let you turn me-o into toothpicks!" Moody wailed. He was making sobbing sounds, but no tears fell from the puppet's glass eyes.

Garmadon held on tight to Moody as he ran back to Hana's house. Hana and her grandmother followed Garmadon into the kitchen, and they surrounded Moody as Garmadon put him down on the floor.

Moody jumped up, ran to the door, and reached for the door handle.

"Let me out! Let me out-io!" he cried. "I won't let you chop me up for firewood!"

"We're not going to hurt you," Garmadon promised. "We just need some information."

"Speak for yourself," Obachan snapped. "I could use a nice new salad bowl."

"Nooooooooooooo!" Moody yelled. "I don't want to be a salad bowl!"

"Then you'd better talk to us," Garmadon said. "Who is Tanabrax? And what exactly did he do to my brother?"

Moody stopped crying and started laughing. "Ha, ha! The boss-io put his soul in a puppet! Your brother's now one of the boss-io's minions!"

"Like you?" Hana asked.

"NO!" Moody shouted angrily. "I'm not a minion. Bunch and I are his number-one and number-two puppets."

"Bunch is the other one," Garmadon explained to Hana and Obachan. He turned to the puppet, "So which one are you? Number one or number two?"

Moody frowned. "Bunch is number one," he replied. "That's what he says, anyway. He always tells me what to do."

"Your name is Moody, right?" Garmadon asked.

Moody started to cry again. "Yes. I'm Moody."

"I wonder why they call you that," Hana muttered under her breath.

Garmadon knelt and looked into Moody's red eyes. "All right, Moody. Start at the beginning. Are you saying that Tanabrax kidnaps people and turns them into puppets?"

"Yes," Moody replied. "But don't tell the boss-io that you heard it from me, because he'll—"

Hana interrupted him. "My brother! Is that what happened to my brother?"

"If you mean that guy we kidnapped from this house-io, then he's a puppet, too," Moody replied.

Hana lunged at him, but Garmadon jumped up and stopped her.

"We've got to get him to talk," Garmadon whispered. "It's the only way to save them."

Hana nodded and backed away.

Garmadon knelt again. "How does Tanabrax do it?"

"If I tell you, will you let me leave?" Moody asked.

Garmadon knew he probably wouldn't let Moody go if it could help him save Wu. But Moody didn't know that. "Sure," he lied.

"Fine," Moody said. "The way Tanabrax tells it, he was a puppeteer a long time ago. One day, a chariot crashed through his traveling puppet stand-io. But it wasn't just any chariot. It was a *djinn* chariot."

"What's that?" Hana asked.

Garmadon explained. "The djinn are mystical beings. I thought I heard Tanabrax speaking djinn in his lair when he stole Wu's soul. Father taught us about the djinn because they can be a powerful enemy."

"And they have powerful magic-io," Moody piped up. "When the chariot crashed through, a magical medallion fell out."

Garmadon gasped. "The one Tanabrax wears around his neck with the spiral in it!"

Moody nodded. "That's the one. Tanabrax picked it up and put it on-io. He felt like it was payment for his ruined stand. Then he sort of became obsessed with it. He sought out big rare books and learned the ancient language of the djinn. Then he figured out how to use the medallion. It can steal souls."

Hana gasped. "That's horrible!"

"Yeah, it's nasty, but it worked out pretty sweet-io for me and Bunch," Moody said. "Tanabrax practiced using the medallion on us first. We were just petty thieves back then, but now we're big-time bad guys! When Tanabrax takes over the world, Bunch and I will be ruling right by his side."

Sounds like a scam to me, Garmadon thought, *but that's not my problem.* He slowly paced back and forth, thinking. "What about all those other puppets? Wu and I heard you talking. Tanabrax has them under some kind of magical control?"

"Yes-io!" Moody replied. "You see, Bunch and I pledged our souls to Tanabrax. We obey him because we want to. But other folks aren't as important as me and Bunch. The boss-io controls their minds so they'll do what we say."

"You're awful!" Hana wailed. "How could you to do this to all those innocent people? What happens to their bodies after Tanabrax takes their souls?"

Moody looked sad. "They sort of just go into a magical sleep-io. And after a few years, they just fade away. . . ."

The puppet's voice trailed off, and Garmadon had a disturbing feeling that Moody's own human body was long gone. He almost felt sorry for the little guy—until he remembered that Moody and his pal were accessories to the extremely evil Tanabrax. But Garmadon still didn't understand something.

"What does Tanabrax want the souls for? And why is he putting them into puppets?"

Moody laughed. "Well, the puppet idea was his, because a soul in a puppet body can live forever."

"An immortal army," Obachan said thoughtfully.

"Right-io!" Moody replied. "See, the medallion's energy is evil. So wearing the medallion has transformed Tanabrax over the years. He used to look like a regular man-io, but now he's mostly made of darkness. That's why he has to live underground. He can't stand the sunlight."

Garmadon tucked this fact away.

"Tanabrax is making a huge puppet army so he can become the most powerful evil guy in Ninjago," Moody continued. "And when that happens, Bunch and I will be living large-io!"

"Ha!" Hana laughed. "You mean living *short*, don't you?"

Moody began to kick his feet and cry. "Why do you have to be so meeaaaaan?" he sobbed.

Hana rolled her eyes. "Seriously? You kidnapped my brother and turned him into a puppet!"

"He won't be a puppet for long," Garmadon said, determined. "And neither will Wu and the others. I have an idea."

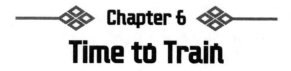

Chapter 6
Time to Train

"Wait! Aren't you going to let me go?" Moody cried.

"Later," Garmadon promised. "Obachan and Hana can keep an eye on you here. You can leave after I defeat Tanabrax and rescue my brother and the others."

Hana put her hands on her hips. "Running off right now isn't going to do any good. Wu, Shin, and many people from this village are literally *puppets* right now. How is defeating Tanabrax going to help them?"

"I'll figure all that out when I get there," Garmadon said, and he moved toward the door.

Obachan held up a hand. "You heard the little man. Tanabrax cannot stand sunlight. We must wait until sunrise to attack."

"What do you mean, 'we'?" Garmadon asked. "I'm the only ninja here."

"You cannot do this alone," Obachan said. "Now that we know what we're up against, we can convince the villagers to help us fight."

Garmadon snorted. "I'm a ninja. How can a bunch of farmers and dumpling makers help take down a bad guy like Tanabrax?"

Moody piped up. "Oh, can't you see-io? You'll need help to get past the puppet army. Then you'll probably want to get the medallion away from Tanabrax, or else you'll become a puppet, too." Then he frowned and

started to cry. "Why did I tell you that? I shouldn't be helping you. I should be helping the boss-io!"

Obachan approached Moody. "You're a smart little fellow, aren't you?"

Moody stopped crying and smiled. "Really-o? You think so? Bunch always calls me a blockhead."

"I'm sure you want to show your friend how smart you are, don't you?" Obachan asked.

Moody nodded. "I sure would-io!"

"Then we will keep our word. You are free to go," Obachan said. "But we hope you will stay and help us instead. We need you, Moody. You are our number-one puppet."

Moody smiled. "Number one? Really?"

Garmadon faced Obachan. "What are you doing?" he hissed. "If he runs way, he's going to tell Tanabrax our plan."

"We need this puppet's brains," she replied. "He's not going to run away. Are you, Moody?"

Moody sobbed. "I'm so confused! I swore an oath to the boss-io. But he and Bunch are always mean to me. How can I leave-io when you're being so nice to me!"

"You don't have to decide now, Moody," Obachan assured him. "Just stay with us for now. If you want to go back to your boss, we'll let you."

Moody nodded. "Ok-io!"

Obachan smirked at Garmadon. "You see?"

"There's no time to waste!" Hana interrupted impatiently. "Let's go wake up some villagers!"

Obachan grabbed a cooking pot and spoon. "Leave it to me."

They followed her outside. Obachan banged the spoon against the pot.

"Wake up! Wake up, everyone! Let's go save our loved ones! Now is the time!"

❖ ❖ ❖

An hour later, two dozen villagers had lined up in a field on the village outskirts. They had all lost friends and relatives to Tanabrax, and now that they knew what was happening, they wanted to help. Along with Hana and Obachan, there were men and women, young people and old. And they were ready to learn.

While Hana and Obachan had gathered the volunteers, Garmadon had squeezed more information out of Moody. The little puppet loved to talk and didn't seem to realize he was giving Garmadon details that could help him fight Tanabrax.

Now Garmadon paced back and forth in front of the villagers, explaining his plan.

"The puppets are made of wood, so they don't feel anything," he explained. "But they can be broken or damaged, and we don't want to do that. Moody told me that if a puppet is destroyed, the soul escapes and you can't get it back. So we can't hurt the puppets. You just need to keep them busy while I handle Tanabrax."

"How do we do that?" one of the villagers asked.

Garmadon turned to a puppet dummy he'd made out of a grain sack and hay. He'd drawn red eyes, a frowny face, and blue hair on it.

"Why does that look like me?" Moody asked.

"That's not important," Garmadon replied. "Now, Wu and I were able to fight off the puppets, but we're trained ninja. You're all going to need some practice."

He delivered a fast low kick to the puppet dummy's knees. The dummy flew backward, and Moody winced, watching it.

"Start with short, swift low kicks," Garmadon explained. He pointed to a knee-high wood fence over by the edge of the field. "Imagine each fence post is a puppet. Now attack!"

The villagers ran to the fence and began kicking the posts. Some of them made contact, but Garmadon was

surprised to see that half of them couldn't even manage a proper kick. One girl just kept kicking the dirt. A farmer kicked and then fell flat on his back. Garmadon shook his head, sighed, and called them back.

One man looked back at the battered fence. "Um, are we going to fix my fence first, or . . ."

"On to the next move!" Garmadon snapped.

Garmadon stood under a tree. "The puppets are trained in sneak attacks," he explained, and Moody dropped the dummy from a tree branch straight onto Garmadon's shoulders.

"If this happens, you need to eject the puppet with a forceful motion—first lean forward, and then quickly flip your shoulders back!" Garmadon demonstrated, and the dummy went flying backward—and quite accidentally knocked Moody out of the tree.

"Ouch-io!" Moody cried, but he jumped back to his feet.

The villagers took turns letting Moody drop the dummy on them and tossing off the dummy. Hana sent the dummy flying farther than anyone else. And Obachan's swift reactions surprised Garmadon.

But some of the villagers were still having trouble. Moody dropped the dummy on one guy, who dropped to the ground and started wrestling it. Garmadon sighed again.

"I've got another idea," he said. "Does everybody have a broom they can use, or a gardening tool with a long handle?"

The villagers scrambled and returned with brooms, shovels, and garden rakes.

"If a puppet attacks you, just whack it with your broom. Like this!" Garmadon demonstrated on the dummy. "Can you at least do *that*?"

The villagers were more successful this time, although some of them ended up whacking each other with the brooms. Garmadon walked over to Obachan and Hana. "I don't think this is going to work."

"At the very least, we can distract the puppet army," Obachan told them.

"I guess you're right," Garmadon said. He turned back to the other volunteers.

"Just one more thing." He pointed to a wooden arch covered in vines.

"Moody, please step through the arch," Garmadon instructed.

"Oh, that's all?" Moody asked. "Sure!"

He stepped through the arch—and into a snare, just like the one that Garmadon and Wu had stepped into the night before. It snapped him up and hung him upside down from the top of the arch.

"No fair!" Moody wailed.

"The snares used by the puppets to set traps are made of incredibly thin thread. They're practically

invisible," Garmadon explained. "But Obachan figured out a way we can spot them."

Obachan walked up to upside-down Moody and held out her palm. She blew on a small pile of flour and it clung to the snare, making it visible.

"We'll use the flour method as we move closer to the lair," Garmadon explained.

Suddenly, the sound of a rooster's crow filled the air. Garmadon gazed at the sky, where the first rays of morning sunlight were peeking over the horizon.

"It's time," he said. "Let's go rescue my brother—and the rest!"

"Hooray!" the villagers cheered.

"Hey!" Moody cried, still stuck in the trap. "Don't leave me hanging!"

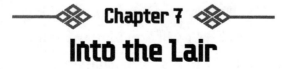

Chapter 7

Into the Lair

Garmadon cut Moody loose and then led the villagers into the woods. Obachan approached him.

"Here," she said, and she handed him a small, round mirror.

"Uh, thanks," Garmadon said. "But the grateful gift-giving usually happens after the ninja save the day."

"You might be able to use this mirror when you face Tanabrax," Obachan told him.

"Why? To scare the enemy with his own reflection?" Garmadon quipped.

Obachan sighed. "Is everything a joke to you? You told us that the medallion glows with light when he uses it. All mirrors reflect light. When he tries to use his medallion on you, use the mirror. Who knows? It might reflect the spell back on him, too."

Garmadon tucked the mirror into his pocket. "Don't worry, he won't get a chance to use the medallion on me. But thanks."

Moody walked up to Obachan. "We're going back to the boss-io now? I still don't know what to do."

"Just imagine, Moody," Obachan said. "Think how impressed Bunch will be when he sees that you are our number-one puppet. He won't be able to boss you around anymore."

"Or bop me on the head," Moody added. "Or threaten to sharpen my head and turn me into a pencil. Or call me blockhead."

Obachan nodded in sympathy. "How did you put up with that all these years?"

Moody shrugged. "I didn't really have a choice. I had to stick with Bunch to get the payoff."

"How long ago did Tanabrax promise you that you'd be ruling the world with him?" she asked.

Moody sighed. "A long, long time ago."

Obachan patted him on the back. "I'm sorry that your boss hasn't kept his promise to you," she told him. "I don't think you owe him any loyalty. But that's your choice, Moody."

"My choice?" Moody asked. "Bunch and the boss-io always tell me what to do."

"Maybe it's time for you to be your own boss. . . ." Obachan's voice trailed off.

The village commando had reached the stand of gnarled black trees. Some of the volunteers held back.

"This place is really spooky," one said.

"Maybe we're not ready for this," added another.

Hana faced them. "Our friends and family need us! We're not backing down now."

Garmadon motioned for everyone to quiet down.

"We're getting closer to the lair," he said. "And I think Tanabrax is probably expecting us."

There was a rustling sound in the trees overhead, and Hana looked up.

"Puppets!" she yelled.

Three dozen puppets dropped down from the trees, landing on the shoulders of six of the villagers. They began punching the villagers and smacking them with wooden clubs.

"Remember your training!" Garmadon yelled.

The villagers flung the puppets off them and sent them flying. The puppets jumped to their feet and charged the villagers, shaking their clubs.

"Puppet kick!" Garmadon cried, and the villagers kicked at the puppets, holding them at bay.

"Now keep them busy," Garmadon ordered. "The rest of you, let's move!"

They ran through the trees. More puppets dropped and more villagers fell back, battling the puppets.

Suddenly, something whizzed past Garmadon's ear. It fell to the ground and he picked it up—a tiny arrow.

"Huh?" He looked down at Moody. "Arrows too? You didn't mention anything about arrows."

Moody shrugged. "I've never seen them before! The boss-io must be trying something new."

"Great!" Garmadon muttered.

Hana scanned the forest. Then she pointed. "They're shooting at us from the top of that flat rock over there!"

Obachan held her broom out in front of her. "I've got this. Hana, keep going with Garmadon and Moody. The rest of you, follow me."

Then she ran toward the rock, shielding herself from the arrows with the bristles of her broom.

"Chaaaaaaarge!"

Garmadon, Hana, and Moody raced ahead until they reached the door in the forest floor. It was open.

"They're waiting for us," Garmadon said.

Moody stopped in his tracks. "What have I done? Obachan and Hana were so nice to me and made me

feel-io like number one. But when Tanabrax learns I've helped you, I'll be toothpicks! I'll be firewood!"

Garmadon put a finger to his lips. "Shhhh. This might be a trap, but I'm not scared. Wu is inside there somewhere, and I'm going to rescue him. You two can stay back if you want."

"No way," Hana said. "I'm going with you. My brother is in there, too, remember?" She knelt and looked Moody in the eyes.

"You've helped us a lot, Moody," she said. "You're definitely our number-one puppet. But you don't have to go in here. Go hide somewhere. We'll take care of Tanabrax."

Moody frowned. Then he smiled. Then he frowned. Then he smiled. It looked like the little puppet didn't know what to feel. Finally, his mouth stopped in a straight line and he nodded.

"I'm your number-one puppet. I won't hide-io," he said firmly.

"Good for you, Moody," Hana said, and she stepped through the doorway and climbed down. Moody followed her into the hole.

Garmadon climbed down after them. His eyes began to adjust to the gloom.

"We'd better check for snares," Moody whispered.

Hana took some flour from a small pouch hanging from her belt and blew on it. The powdery white grains settled on the floor.

"No snares," she said.

They moved forward a few more steps. Hana blew on the flour again.

"All clear," she reported.

They moved farther into the tunnel. Hana blew the flour into the air a third time.

"*A-choo!*"

A flour-covered puppet stepped out of the darkness. "What's wrong with you?" the puppet yelled.

"Bunch!" Moody cried.

Bunch shook the flour off himself. "Moody! Nice work-io, letting yourself get captured like that. But what else would I expect from a blockhead like you?"

"I'm not a blockhead!" Moody replied. "I'm smart-io. These guys think so. And they asked for my help."

"They're just using you," Bunch said. "Once you're done helping them, they'll build furniture with you. You'll be an ugly footstool-io!"

"That's not true," Hana said. "Moody's been a big help to us. We just want to get our family and friends back the way they were. Then Moody can do whatever he wants."

Moody's eyes glowed. "I can?"

Hana smiled at him. "Sure."

Bunch bopped Moody on the head. "Knock it off-io, you blockhead! Help me battle these two so we can make the boss-io happy."

Moody bopped Bunch on the head. "I'm tired of making the boss-io happy. Maybe I want to be happy-o!"

The two angered puppets lunged and knocked each other over.

Bam! Pow! Oof!

They rolled around on the tunnel floor, fighting.

Garmadon motioned to Hana. "Come on!"

They ran along the rest of the tunnel until they reached the underground lair.

"Where's Tanabrax?" Hana asked.

A figure stepped out of the shadows—not Tanabrax, but a puppet. A puppet as small as the other puppets, with white-blond hair, wearing a ninja gi.

Garmadon gasped. "Wu?" he asked as the puppet came closer. "Wu, it's me, Garmadon. Are you in there? Let me help you!"

The Wu puppet launched into a Spinjitzu tornado!

Chapter 8
Brother vs. Puppet

Wu is attacking me! Garmadon thought. *But how can I fight him as a puppet? I don't want to hurt—*

Bam! Puppet Wu collided into Garmadon, knocking him off his feet. Before Garmadon could react, Wu had picked him up by the ankles and flipped him over.

"How can you be so strong? You're just a log in a wig!" Garmadon yelled, jumping to his feet.

Puppet Wu didn't respond with a funny quip, like ninja Wu would have. His glass eyes stared blankly from his carved wooden face. Then he did a handspring flip and landed in front of Garmadon.

Whack! Whack! Whack! He spun around, pummeling Garmadon with spinning kicks.

"That does it!" Garmadon yelled. He grabbed Puppet Wu by the wrist. *"Hi-yaaaa!"*

He tried to flip Puppet Wu, but the puppet's wooden wrist was thin and slippery, and Garmadon lost his grip. Puppet Wu did three backflips and charged Garmadon again.

This time, Garmadon scooped him up with both arms. Then Puppet Wu chomped down on his wrist and Garmadon let go.

"Ouch!" Garmadon yelled. "What kind of puppet has *teeth?*"

Puppet Wu attacked. Garmadon kicked him away, cringing as his brother's puppet body slammed against the wall of the lair.

"I—I can't fight him," Garmadon said. "It's too risky! If I accidentally destroy the puppet's body, Wu's soul will escape!"

Hana frowned, seeing Garmadon's doubts. Her mind searched for a solution—and found it. She darted across the lair, opened the lid of a wooden trunk, and pulled out the contents.

"Garmadon, use this!" she urged.

Garmadon understood her plan. "Got it!"

He ran over to the open trunk and stood in front of it. Puppet Wu was back on his feet.

"Come get me, Wu!" Garmadon called.

Puppet Wu raced across the lair. When he got close to Garmadon, he jumped up and spun into a kick.

Whoosh! Garmadon swiftly moved left. Puppet Wu jumped right into the wooden trunk.

Slam! Garmadon shut the lid and latched the trunk.

"Nice!" Hana said.

"Thanks for the idea," Garmadon replied.

Puppet Wu began kicking the trunk from the inside.

"Can you stay here and keep an eye on my brother?" Garmadon asked. "I need to find Tanabrax."

Hana pointed. "My guess is he's behind that door."

Garmadon turned to see a door made of black wood with strange symbols carved into it.

"Right," Garmadon said.

Then they heard a commotion from the tunnel— the sound of lots and lots of tiny feet.

"That sounds like the puppets," Hana said. "Better hurry!"

Garmadon moved to the door and stepped into a room lit with white candles burning in candelabras. In the flickering light, he could make out what looked like people—rows of them—sleeping on cots. A sparkly, magical-looking mist hung over them.

He looked closer and realized something. The people looked like the puppets. There was the farmer and his wife, the old man, and the boy who looked like Hana.

Moody's words came back to him. *They sort of go into a magical sleep-io. And after a few years, they just fade away.*

Panicked, Garmadon looked for Wu. Then he saw his brother, lying motionless on a cot, his eyes closed. Garmadon ran over and shook him.

"Wu! Wu! Are you all right?"

A laugh echoed through the room, a cold, evil laugh that made the hairs on Garmadon's neck stand on end.

He turned to see Tanabrax, his strange eyes glowing, and the tendrils of his shadowy form slowly waving.

"Fix them!" Garmadon yelled. "You hear me? Fix them all, right now!"

Tanabrax laughed again. "But I did fix them. Their souls will live forever in their puppet forms."

"That's no way to live!" Garmadon cried. He looked back at his brother and wondered if Moody's story had been right. "What will—what will happen to his body?"

"In time it will turn into shadow and blow away with the wind," Tanabrax replied.

"You have to put their souls back," Garmadon said. "I'll make you do it!"

He began to spin. *"Ninjaaaaaaaaaago!"*

He charged toward Tanabrax—and passed right through him!

It's like going through fog, Garmadon thought. *He may have been human once, but he's not anymore! How am I supposed to beat him?*

Tanabrax laughed. "Don't you see, ninja? There is no way to defeat me. You cannot conquer shadow!"

Then—*bam!* An army of puppets burst through the door, carrying some of the tied-up volunteers from

the village commando over their heads. Garmadon looked for Obachan and Moody but didn't see them. Bunch stepped forward.

"I've got more souls for you, boss!" he said proudly.

"Excellent!" Tanabrax said. "But first, I must capture the soul of this ninja so he can join his brother."

Tanabrax held out the medallion and pointed it at Garmadon. It began to glow.

Then he started to chant, and Garmadon recognized the sinister sound of the djinn language—they were the same words Tanabrax had uttered when he'd stolen Wu's soul!

Chapter 9
The Medallion

Hana ran into the dimly lit room and saw what was happening. "Garmadon! Use Obachan's mirror!" she called.

Garmadon reached for the mirror and held it in front of him. Just as Obachan had said, all mirrors reflect light—and the magic light from the medallion reflected back at Tanabrax. He frowned.

"Do you think you can hurt me with my own magic?" he growled. But his eyes began to go blank and his speech became slower. "You . . . do . . . not . . . have . . . the knowledge . . . to . . . use it."

"Maybe not, but at least *you* won't be able to use it anymore," Garmadon shot back.

In a flash, Garmadon leapt up and sailed through the air. Tanabrax's shadowy tentacles reached for him, but the ninja dodged them. He stretched out an arm as far as he could and yanked the medallion from around Tanabrax's neck. It immediately stopped glowing.

Now Garmadon was safe from the medallion's evil powers. Tanabrax spun around and faced Garmadon.

"Give me back that medallion!" he demanded. His eyes flashed an angry red, and the shadowy tentacles once again snaked toward Garmadon. The ninja had his back up against the wall—there was no escape.

"No way!" Garmadon cried. "Now tell me how to fix my brother and all these other people!"

"Never!" Tanabrax yelled. "I will continue to build my puppet army, and no one will be able to stop us!"

Tanabrax can't steal souls anymore, but he's still as powerful as before! Garmadon thought. *Maybe he's right. There's no way to fight a shadow. . . .*

Tanabrax's arms wrapped around Garmadon's chest—and they felt as cold as ice. The ninja gasped for air, and his fingers lost their grip on the medallion. It clattered to the floor. One of Tanabrax's leg tendrils crawled toward it. . . .

"Not so fast!"

It was Obachan. She plowed through the army of puppets, carrying Moody.

"Now, Obachan!" Moody cried.

Obachan tossed Moody into the air. He sailed up, over the head of Tanabrax, and grabbed a handle in the ceiling.

Bunch tried to jump up to stop him. "No, Moody. Not the hatch-io!"

Moody smiled. "I'm no blockhead!" he said, and he yanked on the handle and tumbled to the ground.

Sunlight streamed through the open hatch and hit Tanabrax.

"Nooooooooo!" he wailed.

Tanabrax's tendrils curled back toward his body. Garmadon felt the air rush back into his lungs. He quickly picked up the dropped medallion.

Tanabrax's body began to dissolve into wisps of smoke. His eyes widened in shock.

"No!" he cried. "This can't be happening!"

Then his face dissolved, too. The smoke swirled and then shot up through the hatch in the ceiling.

Hana ran over to Obachan and hugged her. "You did it, Grandma!"

"Hey, don't forget about me," Garmadon said. He held up the medallion.

Bunch marched up to Moody and started screaming at him. "What did you do that for?" he yelled. "What are we supposed to do without the boss-io?"

Moody nodded toward the puppets. "Um, I think we've got a bigger problem to worry about first."

The puppets had all lost the dazed look in their eyes. They were looking around the lair, confused. Then they looked down at their wooden bodies.

"What's going on?" the Farmer Uchida puppet asked.

"I'm made of wood!" cried Old Man Jiro.

Hana's brother ran up to her. "Hana, what's wrong with us? What's happened to me?"

Then Garmadon heard the muffled voice of his brother from the other room.

"Get me out of here! Help! Help!"

"Wu!" Garmadon cried, and he raced over to the wooden chest and opened it. Puppet Wu climbed out.

"Garmadon!" Puppet Wu cried. "Tanabrax turned me into a—"

"A puppet, I know," his brother replied. We took care of Tanabrax, but, um, now we have to figure out how to get your soul back into your body."

"My body!" Puppet Wu said. "Where is it? Is it okay?"

"In the other room," Garmadon said, and Puppet Wu hurried past him, running on his tiny legs. Garmadon couldn't help it—he laughed.

Wu spun around. "What's so funny?"

"You're kind of cute this way," Garmadon said. "Are you sure you want your body back? We could come up with a great ventriloquist act together. I bet we could be famous."

"There is nothing funny about this," Wu said, and he marched into the other room.

All the puppets were standing by their bodies, staring sadly at them. Hana leaned over her sleeping brother, and Obachan wrung her hands.

"What are we going to do?" she asked. "We can't leave them like this."

"Why not?" Bunch piped up. "Moody and I have been puppets for years and years and years. It's not so bad-io."

Puppet Wu walked over to the puppet henchmen.

"When Tanabrax stole my soul, I heard him say some words," Puppet Wu said, and he shuddered at the memory of his soul leaving his body. "They were in the djinn language, right?"

"That's right-io," Bunch responded. "The medallion used to belong to the djinn."

"How did he learn their language? Did he have a book?" Puppet Wu asked.

Moody's eyes lit up. "He did! A special book-io! I know where it is!"

He quickly ran off and returned with a book that had a purple leather cover and gold-edged pages. He handed it to Puppet Wu.

Puppet Wu opened it, and Garmadon looked over his shoulder anxiously.

"The book is all in the djinn language!" Garmadon exclaimed. "How are we supposed to figure it out?"

"There are pictures," Puppet Wu said. "Pictures always make things easier. Besides, I remember the words Tanabrax said when he took my soul."

Puppet Wu leafed through the pages of the book. Then he stopped.

"Here!" Puppet Wu said, pointing. "This is a picture of a soul leaving a body, and these are the words that Tanabrax said. And on the next page, there's a picture of a soul returning to a body. So these must be the right words to say."

"How do you know for sure?" Garmadon asked.

"I don't," Puppet Wu replied. "But what's the worst that could happen?"

Bunch pointed to some words on the page. "I know a little bit of the djinn language from listening to the boss-io. These words mean '*all* souls.' So all souls will return to their bodies if you use this spell. The only problem is . . ."

"Bunch and I don't have our bodies anymore," Moody finished. "They disappeared a long time ago."

"That means you can't do the spell-io!" Bunch cried. "It'll be the end of me and blockhead here!"

Moody looked at Bunch. "You know, Bunch, we've been puppets for a very long time," he said. Then he looked at the bodies. "When we got turned into puppets, we didn't have a lot to live for. But these people, they've got friends. And brothers and sisters and moms and dad-ios."

Obachan stepped over to them. "It's your decision," she said. "But please think of the others who haven't had such a long run as you, boys. Let my grandson grow up to live a happy life. Let Farmer Uchida go back to his fields."

Bunch frowned. "I . . . I like being a puppet."

"It's been fun-io, Bunch," Moody said. "But it's not all it's cracked up to be. I miss an awful lot of things . . . like being able to smell flowers, or taste noodles."

"And snuggling up with a furry kitty-o," Bunch added with a sigh.

Moody nodded. "I'm not sure what will happen if they cast that spell-io. Maybe it'll be a new adventure. Something even better than this."

Bunch sighed. "You're right-io. I don't know what I'll do without the boss-io anyway." He turned to look up at Garmadon and Wu. "Cast the spell!"

Obachan hugged both puppets. "Thank you," she said softly.

Garmadon took the book from his brother. "We have to try," he said. "Wu, get over to your body."

Puppet Wu hurried to his human body. Hana stayed by her puppet brother's side.

Obachan looked at Garmadon. "Do it, ninja. I know that you can."

Her words gave him confidence. Garmadon held up the medallion like he'd seen Tanabrax do. Then he said the words in the djinn language as loudly as he could.

Nothing happened at first, and Garmadon's heart quickly sank.

But then the medallion began to glow. And it began to spin. Garmadon watched as golden light flowed out of the mouths of the puppets and into the mouths of the sleeping humans.

When all the golden light was gone, the glow in the medallion faded. An eerie silence filled the lair. Then the puppets fell limply to the floor in a clatter.

The sparkling mist above the bodies dissolved. The humans began to slowly sit up.

"Hana! Grandma!" Shin cried, and he stood and hugged them both.

Garmadon walked over to Wu. "How do you feel?" he asked.

"Stiff," Wu responded as he stretched. "And hungry!"

Then he looked over at Moody and Bunch. The two puppets were slowly fading away.

"Moody!" Hana cried, and she ran to him.

"Bye, Hana! Bye, Obachan!" the puppet called with a big smile on his face. "Thanks for being so nice to me!"

Then the puppets dissolved into a dust that swirled around the room and floated out the hatch in the ceiling.

Hana wiped a tear from her eye. "I'm going to miss that little guy."

"I will, too," Obachan agreed. "They may have been bad, but they did the right thing in the end."

She turned to the kidnapped humans and clapped her hands. "Everyone—come back to our village and we will feed you. If you are not from around here, we will help you get home."

They all began to file out of the dark lair. Hana approached Garmadon and Wu.

"Um, what should we do with all these puppets?" she asked, looking at the wooden replicas of the villagers scattered around. "I mean, they're not really alive anymore, right?"

"Maybe we'll just leave them here," Garmadon said. "Although, I'd love to bring that Wu puppet home to show Father. He'll never believe—"

Garmadon stopped. The Wu puppet wasn't near the cot. Garmadon looked under and around it.

"Wu, your puppet's gone," Garmadon said.

Wu sighed. "Yeah, right, I'm not in the mood for jokes right now," he replied, but then he saw the serious look on his brother's face. "That's impossible. It couldn't just walk away."

Their eyes traveled to the ceiling, where sunlight streamed through the open hatch.

"I'm sure it's around here somewhere," Garmadon said, but he didn't sound convinced.

"Yeah, right," Wu said, more hesitantly this time. "Come on, let's go get some food!"

They followed the others out of the lair.

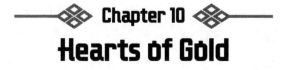

Chapter 10

Hearts of Gold

Back outside, Garmadon and Wu rolled a big rock over the opening in the ground. Then everyone headed into the woods full of black trees.

When they reached the village, those who hadn't joined the fight ran out of their homes.

"We rescued everyone!" Obachan announced. "But none of our loved ones would be back with us here if it weren't for two brave puppets named Bunch and Moody. They may have been made of wood, but they certainly had hearts of gold."

"Cheers to Bunch and Moody!" Hana cried.

"Cheers to Bunch and Moody!" the grateful villagers chanted.

Then Obachan instructed everyone to prepare food for a feast, and they ran into their homes. Hana and Shin approached Garmadon and Wu.

"We really need to thank you," she said. "If you hadn't come to our village, I never would have gotten my brother back. I don't know what I would have done without him."

Garmadon looked over at Wu. "I know what you mean."

Wu's eyes went wide. "Did I just hear right? Did you just say something nice about me?"

"Don't push it," Garmadon said.

Then Wu's face got serious. "You know, we need to do something about that medallion," he said. "Djinn magic is nothing to mess around with. Maybe we should return it to them."

Garmadon laughed. "That might be your worst idea ever, and you've had some pretty bad ones. Messing with the djinn is the last thing we need to do right now. We need to eat, sleep, and then pack up supplies and get back on our journey."

Wu nodded. "You're right, brother. But what about the medallion?"

"I will take care of it."

The brothers turned to see Obachan behind them.

"That's nice, Obachan," Garmadon said. "But how can we make sure you won't let it get into the wrong hands?"

"Follow me," she said, and she led Garmadon and Wu back to her garden. She picked up a shovel and dug a hole.

"Fetch the flour crock from the kitchen," Obachan instructed, and Wu quickly obeyed. Obachan dropped the medallion into the ceramic crock and put it in the hole. Then she dropped a potted flower into the hole and filled it up with dirt.

"The flowers will grow over it. Nobody will ever think to look for it here."

"Are you *sure* it will be safe?" Wu asked nervously.

Everything Obachan had done in the past twenty-four hours flashed through Garmadon's mind. Leading the charge to train the villagers. Hurling Moody toward the hatch.

"I'm pretty sure it will, Wu," he said. "Thank you, Obachan."

"You're welcome," she said. She stood up and leaned the shovel against a fence. "Now let's go eat some of Mrs. Uchida's dumplings. They're not as good as mine, but they'll fill you up."

Wu looked at Garmadon and grinned. "Dumplings today, back on the road tomorrow?"

"Sure," Garmadon replied and smiled too. "Our journey can definitely wait for dumplings!"

Epilogue

The six young ninja stared with open mouths at Master Wu as he finished his story. Suddenly, Jay cried, "Look! It's one of those living puppets!"

The others turned to look back.

A wooden puppet with a curly mustache walked down the stone street, headed right toward them.

"Aaaahhhh!" Cole cried. "Its creepy glass eyes are looking right at me! *Hiyyaaaaa!*"

Cole lunged at the puppet, grabbed it, and flung it to the ground.

"Hey, what are you doing?"

Cole looked up to see a man inside a horse-drawn cart. He was holding two pieces of wood put together

make a cross shape, with strings dangling from them
that were attached to the puppet. It was the puppeteer.

"Oh, sorry," Cole said, and he handed the puppet
back to the scowling puppeteer.

The ninja started laughing as they walked up to the
cart. More puppeteers held puppets dressed in colorful
costumes.

"I'm sorry, too," Jay said. "I was just playing a prank on my friend here. Master Wu was telling us a scary story about puppets."

"That's fine," the puppeteer said. "We're doing another show in about twenty minutes. You should come see it. It's a lot of fun. Not scary at all."

"No thanks," Cole said.

"Yeah, um, we've got ninja things to do," Kai said.

"Yes, we really should get going," Nya said.

The wagon moved on, and the ninja walked down the village street.

"Admit it," Cole said. "Master Wu's story spooked all of you!"

Zane nodded. "I will admit it," he said. "If I could have nightmares, those puppets would probably give them to me."

"Oh, great," Nya said. "I'll never be able to sleep tonight!"

Master Wu smiled. "So you understand why I was not interested in seeing a traveling puppet show."

"I wonder whatever happened to that puppet of you, Master Wu," Lloyd said.

Master Wu shrugged. "I'm sure it's still somewhere in that underground lair. I don't really think much about it anymore."

"And Tanabrax was never seen again?" Nya asked.

"Never again," Master Wu replied.

"Except maybe in our nightmares," Nya said with a shudder.

"Maybe we should get more donuts," Cole suggested. "It's always easier to sleep on a full stomach."

"Donuts are good, and family is even better," Lloyd added. "There's nothing to be afraid of when we're together, right?"

"Right!" the ninja agreed.

Laughing and talking, Master Wu and his students walked away from the festival. And in the back of the traveling wagon, a puppet sat up and watched them go. A puppet with glowing glass eyes and no strings . . .

Glossary

Bunch and Moody

Two puppets who loyally serve Tanabrax. In the past, they were petty thieves who wanted to be the villain's best henchmen. They were also the first people he turned into puppets.

Cole

Cole is a member of Master Wu's ninja team. As the Earth Ninja, he wields the elemental power of Earth and supports his friends with his confidence and great physical strength.

Djinn

A mystical being capable of granting wishes. The djinns inhabited a realm called Djinjago.

First Spinjitzu Master

The creator of Spinjitzu and the entire Ninjago world. He was also the father of Garmadon and Wu, whom he trained in the art of Spinjitzu to protect the world he had created.

Garmadon

Wu's older brother and a son of the First Spinjitzu Master. Bitten by a vile snake as a child, Garmadon gradually filled with evil to become Lord Garmadon, the greatest villain in the world of Ninjago.

Gi

A type of clothing traditionally worn by ninja.

Hana

A young, brave girl whose brother, Shin, was captured by Tanabrax's puppets and turned into a puppet, like many other people from her village. Hana wants Garmadon and Wu to help her rescue Shin and the other villagers.

Jay

The Lightning Ninja is quick-witted, talks fast, and often acts before he thinks. Jay also loves pranks and jokes. Without his sense of humor, the ninja team would be in a much worse mood.

Kai

Kai is the Fire Ninja. With his fierce temper, bravery, and strong sense of justice, he'll stop at nothing if he has put his mind to it.

Lloyd

Wise beyond his years, Lloyd is the Green Ninja and the leader of the ninja team. He is the son of Garmadon, the grandson of the First Spinjitzu Master, and Master Wu's nephew.

Nya

Kai's younger sister is the Water Ninja. She's a skilled warrior, inventor, and tech wiz. She's often the team's voice of reason and a steadfast support to her friends on every mission.

Obachan

Hana and Shin's wise grandmother and a respected dumpling vendor. Obachan may look like just another villager, but there's more to her than meets the eye.

Scrolls of Forbidden Spinjitzu

Two scrolls of paper that contain the dark powers of Forbidden Spinjitzu. Although the maker of the scrolls, the First Spinjitzu Master, told his sons never to touch them, young Wu and Garmadon stole them to defeat a Serpentine sorceress called Aspheera.

Spinjitzu

An ancient technique based on balance and rotation in which you tap into your elemental energy while turning quickly. Developed by the First Spinjitzu Master long before time had a name, Spinjitzu is more than a martial art: it's also a way of living. Mastering it is a lifelong journey.

Tanabrax

A mysterious powerful villain, Tanabrax is a creature of shadow, using the dark energy of a djinn's medallion to build his own puppet army to take control over the world of Ninjago.

Wu

Wu is the other son of the First Spinjitzu Master, and little brother to Garmadon. After many years of mastering the art of Spinjitzu and the ways of the ninja, Wu shares his knowledge with his students— Lloyd, Kai, Cole, Jay, Zane, and Nya—to train them as ninja protectors of the world of Ninjago.

Zane

Brave and caring Zane is the Titanium Ninja, wielding the elemental power of ice. He is a Nindroid (ninja robot), created to protect those who cannot protect themselves.